REALITY SHOW

The ISLAND

D. A. GRAHAM

darbycreek
MINNEAPOLIS

Darby Creek
A division of Lerner Publishing Group, Inc.
241 First Avenue North
Minneapolis, MN 55401 USA

For reading levels and more information, look up this title at www.lernerbooks.com.

Image credits: Kyrylo Glivin/Shutterstock.com (feet); pangploy/Shutterstock.com (palms); Pierre-Yves Babelon/Shutterstock.com (shelter).

Main body text set in Janson Text LT Std 12/17.5.
Typeface provided by Adobe Systems

Library of Congress Cataloging-in-Publication Data

Names: Graham, D. A., 1995– author.
Title: The island / D. A. Graham.
Description: Minneapolis : Darby Creek, [2019] | Series: Reality show | Summary: When Ethan, an avid outdoorsman, competes on his favorite reality television program, Teen Wilderness Masters, he quickly learns that he is in over his head.
Identifiers: LCCN 2018027166 (print) | LCCN 2018035120 (ebook) | ISBN 9781541541917 (eb pdf) | ISBN 9781541540286 (lb : alk. paper) | ISBN 9781541545427 (pb : alk. paper)
Subjects: | CYAC: Reality television programs—Fiction. | Wilderness survival—Fiction. | Survival—Fiction. | Competition (Psychology)—Fiction. | Islands—Fiction.
Classification: LCC PZ7.1.G716 (ebook) | LCC PZ7.1.G716 Isl 2019 (print) | DDC [Fic]—dc23

LC record available at https://lccn.loc.gov/2018027166

Manufactured in the United States of America
1-45233-36615-9/17/2018

CHAPTER 1

The boat sped along the ocean waves, kicking foam into my face as I leaned out over the side. My eyes watered as the wind whipped at my face. I blinked the tears away and squinted. I was surrounded by bright blue water. In the distance, I could make out a tiny, dark speck. Our destination.

The island.

Deserted and covered in jungle, the island had no name. The closest town was all the way in Florida, separated from the island by miles of water. It was the perfect location to show off my survival skills.

On the boat with me were nine other teenagers probably thinking exactly the same thing. We were headed to the island to compete on my favorite reality TV show, *Teen Wilderness Masters*, for a grand prize of fifty thousand dollars. On the show, contestants got dropped off in a remote location somewhere around the world with nothing but the clothes on their backs. This season, we were headed to a deserted island in the Caribbean, and for ten days we'd camp, search for our food, and compete against one another in various challenges. And I was going to be the winner—the true Teen Wilderness Master.

I gripped the boat's rail and leaned forward even more, feeling the full force of the wind. It was so much better being outside and not down in the cabin with the other contestants.

"Hey, Ethan! Get down from there!" a man's voice shouted suddenly. "It's dangerous."

I turned to face Chase Hanning, the host of *Teen Wilderness Masters.* He frowned and crossed his arms.

"Sorry, Chase," I said. "I just wanted to get some fresh air."

"If you have to puke, do it off the back of the boat."

I laughed, but Chase wasn't joking. He pointed at the cabin. Holding onto the rail for balance as the boat bounced over the waves, I scooted past him and through the door to the cabin. Chase followed and closed the door behind us, shutting out the howl of the wind.

Once an unknown video blogger, Chase became famous when one of his music videos went viral. Now he hosted *Teen Wilderness Masters* and had sponsorships with all kinds of outdoor apparel companies. I was still a little star-struck around him.

Along with nature documentaries, I grew up watching *Wilderness Masters* and its spin-off, *Teen Wilderness Masters*. But my favorite pastime was exploring the wilderness surrounding my family's Wyoming home. I spent my days watching bison migrate across the plains, newts swim through creeks, and eagles catch fish in the lakes. In order to blend into the nature around me, I learned how to mask my scent, cover my tracks, and create hidden shelters.

My parents were both research biologists and used to take me out in the field with them. They had taught me to find edible plants, to make clean drinking water, and to love all the plants and animals around our home. But then my dad got sick and my mom helped take care of him, so I had to go exploring on my own. A couple years ago he started to recover, but the medical bills were so expensive. My parents couldn't hide how worried they were about money. I decided I would do whatever I could to help. I started spending as much time outside as possible, honing my survival and exploration skills. If I could get a spot on *Teen Wilderness Masters* and win the prize money, then maybe I could help pay off the bills or take my parents on a trip around the world.

Inside the boat's cabin, I looked at the determined faces of my fellow explorers. There were six boys and four girls, each looking fierce in their own way. They were all lean and tough from years spent outdoors. Whatever challenges lay ahead, I would have some serious competition. But I hoped my motivation to win—my family—would bring me to the final round.

"We're nearing the island now, folks," said Chase as I took my seat beside a stony-faced female contestant. "Once we get there, the first round of the competition will begin."

Another girl looking out the window turned her head to Chase. A sly smile flashed across her features, then quickly disappeared.

"This first round is about showcasing your individual survival skills," Chase continued. As he spoke, he reached down and lifted a cushion on the bench beside him. He pulled out a black plastic box about the size of a briefcase. "Each of you will be dropped off in a different place along the shore. It's up to you to find food, water, and shelter—because we aren't coming back for you for three whole days.

"But don't worry. We have cameras hidden all over the island, and each of you will wear a small waterproof camera on your clothes, so if there's an emergency, we can come in and get you."

Chase put the box down on the bench and popped its clasps open. All ten of us leaned forward eagerly. Inside the box were several pieces of fabric, each a different bright color.

"In addition to surviving in the jungle, each of you will have your own flag," Chase said. He plucked out a neon green cloth and unfolded it. It was square, like a bandana, and had the *Teen Wilderness Masters* logo printed in the center. On one corner was a metal clasp. "This flag is like your life force. You must wear it on your hip and have it displayed at all times, out in the open. But do your best to keep it attached to you. Because in order to move on to the next round, you need not just one but two flags. You will have to steal another competitor's flag and protect your own."

I glanced at my competitors. They grinned with excitement. My lips curled into a smile too. *This is going to be fun*, I thought.

"They can be any two flags," Chase continued. "So if you lose yours early on, you can still make a comeback. Other than that, the same *Teen Wilderness Masters* rules apply: no hurting each other, no disabling your camera, and no trying to swim off the island. Florida is very far away!"

A few competitors snickered.

"Oh, one more thing," Chase said. He lifted the black box. "You see this here? There are boxes like this hidden all over the island. They contain different sorts of supplies—food, cooking utensils, blankets—to help you out during this first round."

The girl by the window scoffed. "I thought this was a survival game," she muttered.

"You're free to use as many or as few of these boxes as you'd like," Chase told her cheerfully. "But there won't be any penalties if you do. Now everyone take a flag and look at the number printed on it."

I snatched a light blue one. Right below the metal clasp was a small white 3.

"Who's got number one?" Chase asked.

The girl by the window raised her hand. Her flag was red.

Chase grinned. "You'll be leaving the boat first."

That means I'm third, I thought with relief. That was good—I'd have more time than most of the others to find some of those supply boxes. Even if it was only a difference of a few minutes, I knew that every one of them counted in this game.

When the boat reached the island, the driver cut the motor. The water here was clear and almost green. Window girl stood up and left the cabin with Chase. A few seconds later, there was a splash, and I saw her wade up to the beach.

We went about a quarter mile up the shore and dropped off the second competitor.

Then it was my turn.

I leaped off the back of the boat into the shallow, warm water. A few small fish scattered as I made my way to the beach. The jungle stood in front of me, dark and silent. With my flag at my side and my heart hammering in my chest, I clenched my fists and ran into the darkness.

CHAPTER 2

I was immediately surrounded by walls of green.

On the beach there were only palm trees, but here there were also other tropical trees that looked more like the ones I remembered from home. Their branches spread out high above, making a broad, flat crown of leaves that collected most of the sunlight. Underneath the trees, there were vines sprouting from leafy bushes.

The air was hot and wet. Sweat clung to my skin, and I paused under one of the big trees to catch my breath.

As I rested, I listened for signs of another human being. I heard so many birdcalls I couldn't tell them apart. But no telltale sound of feet stepping over the ground or heavy, human breathing. Apart from my own, of course.

But even though I was apparently alone, I felt like all eyes were on me. I glanced up at the branches above me, seeking one of the hidden cameras Chase mentioned. I didn't see one, so I started fiddling with the small camera Chase had attached to my chest. It was a small black box with no buttons—just a lens.

As I caught my breath, I reviewed my plan of action. I needed to find water first, perhaps by locating a supply box.

I started off, keeping my eyes peeled for the sorts of places a supply box would be. I knew from watching previous seasons of the show that boxes could be hidden inside dead tree trunks, between two rocks, or even out in the open, where someone could easily spot them.

Squinting, I moved from sunshine, to shade, to sunshine again. The shadows cast by the leaves made a polka-dot pattern on the ground.

Except for one the spot where there was a big, square shadow.

I looked up. In a fork in the branches above me was a supply box. It was too high up for me to reach, even on my tiptoes, so I grabbed a fallen branch from nearby and nudged it loose. The box scooted forward and then fell with a huge *BANG!*

Amazingly, it didn't break open. But it did attract the attention of another competitor—a muscular boy with sharp eyes stepped out of the bushes right as I knelt to open the supply box.

I stared at him, and he stared at me. Then we both looked at the box on the ground between us. Then back at each other.

I dropped the branch and ran. I tore through the underbrush, my flag flapping in the wind. I sprinted over tree roots and rocks. And then when I couldn't sprint anymore, I jogged until my heart was slamming so loud in my chest that it was all I could hear. I stopped and looked back, but the boy hadn't followed me. He must have gone for the supplies.

Shoot! I thought. *I could have taken his flag.* I was so scared of losing my own that I forgot he had one too.

I decided to creep back and see if he was still there. If he was distracted by the box, I might be able to take his flag still. But when I got there, the box was split open and totally empty. There was no sign of the boy.

Panting and sweating from my unexpected sprint, I started walking again, this time in a different direction. I needed to find some water—and fast.

***

The sunlight was fading by the time I found another supply box nestled at the roots of a tree. I yanked it free of the vines and, not wanting to run into another competitor, dragged it into the shadows.

I opened it and pulled out a canteen for carrying water along with several water-purification tablets. Under that was a sharp wedge of shiny gray rock that looked like some flint for making fire.

They were all useful things. But I needed shelter, food, and water first. Above me, the sky was turning a deep red. I was running out of time. Searching in the dark would be impossible.

Buried at the bottom of the box was something else too. It was a lumpy piece of wood, about the size of a tennis ball, that had been carved to look like a pig. There were notches for the eyes, mouth, and hooves. I searched its surface for instructions, a riddle, or any other indication for its purpose. But there was nothing.

As I tucked the mysterious pig token into my pocket, I heard a soft *whoosh* in the distance.

A jolt of anticipation shot through me. *Water.*

Following the sound, I rushed through the trees and came across a small stream tumbling down the slope of a hill. I fell to my knees, filled my canteen, and dropped in a tablet.

When I knew it was safe to drink, I guzzled it down. The water was cold and refreshing.

After I drank my fill, I checked out my surroundings. Up the hill a little ways was a rocky cliff with just enough space at the base for me to sleep, protected from both the elements and the eyes of my competitors. I climbed up there and settled against the rocks to sleep.

Tomorrow, I'd make it my mission to find a flag.

CHAPTER 3

I woke up to the sound of heavy breathing and shuffling. But the rocks blocked my view of whoever it was. The heavy breathing turned to snorting as whoever it was stooped to drink from the stream. Crouching behind the rocks, I slowly poked my head over them to see.

I saw nothing but green. No bright pink or orange or red or any other color that a flag might be.

And then I saw it—a tiny pig. It gulped down mouthfuls of water. It had white spots all over its brown fur, like a baby deer.

My stomach growled.

The pig lifted its head and looked right at me.

"Uh, hey," I said.

It bolted into the jungle.

"No!" I cried. I scooped up my flint and chased after the pig. I wasn't a hunter—I loved animals, and I rarely ate meat—but I was starving! I hadn't realized how hungry I was until I imagined bacon roasting over a campfire.

The pig was fast. Squealing, it ducked under huge ferns and scrambled over fallen logs. Ahead of us, a pile of moss-covered rocks appeared in the brush. At the base of the pile was a small cave. The pig raced into the cave.

Nearly crashing into the rocks, I jammed my hand into the cave. I felt the pig's hot breath but couldn't reach it. I swiped a few more times and then sat back and groaned. My stomach ached with hunger.

I can't believe I was outsmarted by a pig.

I lay down on the jungle floor and stared up at the trees. Between the leaves, I got glimpses of blue sky. There were also smaller, darker shapes among the leaves. I squinted. *Berries.*

All around me were huge bushes covered in the little fruits. They looked like tiny plums. I could practically smell their sweetness. My mouth watered.

I sat up and noticed little hoof prints in the soft dirt, as well as squashed, half-eaten berries. *If the pig can eat these berries, then so can I!*

I stuffed my face until the juices made my fingers and chin sticky. Instantly my body felt ready to run across the entire island and back again. It was amazing how much a little food could do. I thought about packing some berries away for later and only then realized that, in the rush to catch the pig, I had left my canteen at my shelter. *Shoot*, I thought. *I hope no one finds it while I'm gone.*

Behind me came the sound of cautious huffing. I glanced over my shoulder and saw the pig had poked its head out of the cave.

"Hey, little guy," I said gently.

It ducked back into the darkness.

I picked up one of my berries and slowly extended my hand toward the opening of the cave. I felt the pig's nose wiggle against my fingertips. Then it took the berry from my fingers. A few berries later, I had successfully coaxed the pig from the cave. It sat on the dirt in front of me.

"Do you want some more berries?" I said, standing up. The pig backed away, nervous, but I showed it I meant it no harm by plucking some berries from the tops of the bushes and putting them on the ground for it to eat.

As the pig ate, a strange scent wafted into my nose. The scent of something cooking. My stomach growled again, and the pig glanced up at me.

"I'll be right back," I told it and got up to follow the smell. It had to be another competitor. This time, I wouldn't run away.

I crept through the jungle and soon stumbled upon the edge of a clearing. In the middle of the clearing was a fish roasting over a campfire. Sitting by the fire, facing away from me, was the first girl that jumped from the boat. Her red flag stood out in the middle of the green backdrop. She was in the process of weaving a sack out of palm tree leaves.

I decided to sneak up on her and snatch her flag while she was distracted. I took a step toward her camp.

Suddenly, I was swept off my feet.

I yelped with surprise as my left leg flew into the air, lifted by a vine toward the treetops. I lost my balance and hit the dirt. The flint tumbled out of my pocket to the ground. I wasn't fully upside down, but my left leg was stuck in midair and wouldn't come down no matter how hard I pulled. I scraped at the dirt, looking for something—anything—to help, but instead I found a pair of blue sneakers. I looked up at the girl.

She smirked. "Well, you aren't a pig."

"That's true," I said.

She reached out toward me. But instead of helping me down, she plucked my flag from my hip like a berry from a bush.

"Hey!" I protested. "That's mine."

"Not anymore," she said, attaching it to her other hip. She started to walk away.

"Wait. Aren't you going to cut me loose?"

"Yeah, right. You'll just try to steal your flag back," she laughed. "What was your name again? Ethan? Look, Ethan, if you can't get yourself out of a simple snare trap, then maybe you shouldn't be on *Teen Wilderness Masters*."

How rude. I tried swinging my body to see if that would loosen the vine, but it only made it tighter. "What's your name?" When it became clear she wouldn't answer, I tried a different approach. "Do you normally go around setting traps for people?"

"It's for pigs. Or deer and coyotes, which is what I'm used to hunting back in Montana. And my name is Amanda."

"Did you get that fish from a supply box?"

"No way! I don't need the producers to help me get food or shelter. I know how to do all that on my own."

"So you're a purist?" I asked.

She shrugged.

There was always someone like her on each season of *Teen Wilderness Masters*, someone who refused to use the supplies given to them by the show. The fans started calling them survival purists. I respected the purists because it took a lot of skill to survive without any help.

I wasn't a purist. I liked exploring, and I couldn't always explore everything unless I had a compass or some rope for climbing rocks or some food packed away so I didn't have to worry about finding it on my own. That gave me more time to focus on the animals. I explained this to the girl while trying to bounce myself loose. She just shrugged again, but she smiled as she watched me make a fool of myself.

That was a good sign. *If I can't convince her to free me, then maybe I can convince her I'm just a harmless jokester*, I thought. *She'll let down her guard, and we can become allies.*

"I live in Wyoming, so we're basically neighbors," I went on. "My parents are biologists, and they do lots of research on endangered animals. They're trying to prevent vulnerable species from going extinct."

"That's really cool," she said. "It's important to protect the wildlife. I want to help endangered animals when I get older too."

"So do I. Maybe we'll get to work together someday!" I beamed.

She crossed her arms. "Now I feel a little guilty for stealing your flag. But I can't give it back to you, either, because I want to win the game."

"You could give me some of that fish," I suggested.

She raised an eyebrow. But then she brought over the cooked fish for us to share. I was still hanging by one foot from a tree and she kept my flag on her hip. So we were friendly, I decided, but not yet allies.

Finally, Amanda packed up her camp. She saluted me, and before she vanished into the jungle, she gave me some advice: "Use the flint to cut yourself loose."

Oh. Duh.

CHAPTER 4

After I cut myself out of the trap, I tried to follow Amanda to steal back my flag. But I couldn't find her anywhere. She had truly vanished.

As I explored, I found abandoned campsites from last night: signs that other competitors had been near here. And, in a stroke of luck, I stumbled upon an unopened supply box that held cans of beans, tuna, and pineapple.

That night, I returned to my shelter under the overhang, started a small fire using the flint, and cooked the strangest meal I'd eaten in a long time. My canteen was still there, which was a good sign that no one else had found my camp.

As I ate, I saw a glint of gold in the trees across the stream. I squinted but couldn't see what it was.

I glanced around, hoping no one was watching. Then I darted out of my shelter and across the stream. Tucked in the underbrush was what looked like a supply box, but it was smaller and painted gold. A padlock dangled from it. I picked it up, but it was way heavier than I expected. I looked all around for a key, but I only found one of the show's hidden cameras. It was in a tree, disguised as a clump of leaves. Whatever this golden box was, it was clearly important. But it was too heavy for me to lug around during the rest of the competition. *My priority needs to be getting flags.*

I buried the chest in some leaves so no one else would find it.

***

The next day was my last chance to get a pair of flags. I collected all my supplies and set out to track down some competitors. As the sun peeked through the treetops, I suddenly had an idea.

I returned to the location of Amanda's old camp and studied the trap that had caught me. She had taken a thin but strong vine from a tree, threw it over a branch, and tied a counterweight to one end. The other end had a loop on it that would go on the ground. When I stepped into the loop, the counterweight fell, pulling the loop shut and causing the end attached to me to fly upward.

I repaired the vine and reset the trap, covering it in leaves to hide it. It took about an hour to set up. The sun crawled higher in the air. Time was running out.

For the final touch, I started a fire and started cooking the rest of my food out in the open. Maybe it was a long shot. But it worked on me, so there was a good chance it would work on someone else.

And that's exactly what happened.

After about an hour, another competitor appeared out of nowhere. One moment I saw nothing but trees. The next, the trees seemed to be walking. A neon yellow flag dangled off the hip of this supposed tree. I realized this competitor had completely coated herself in mud and leaves to hide herself better. She had to leave the flag exposed, but it was good camouflage. If I hadn't been paying attention, I would have missed her.

I quickly looked back at the cooking food, pretending not to see her. She stalked toward me, confident in her disguise. But my—or, Amanda's—trap was disguised even better. Up went the girl's foot. She yelped and started thrashing. I laughed as I approached.

"You jerk," she snarled. "Peter! Peter, help!"

Right as I took her flag, someone else appeared, a bright pink flag on his waist. He was coated in mud and leaves too.

"Jessie, what—" he started, then he saw me. His eyes widened in surprise.

My heart pounded. I hadn't counted on this. I hadn't thought anyone would have already formed an alliance. My legs tensed up, ready to bolt into the trees, but I resisted. I had run away once before, from Muscle Dude, and it was a wasted opportunity. This time, I wasn't going to let a flag get away.

Peter was a large boy, both tall and wide. He loomed over me.

I charged right at him.

Peter yelped and instinctively raised his arms to protect himself as I crashed into him. We both collapsed, me on top of him. I ripped his flag from his waist and stood up, triumphant, each of my hands enclosed over a neon flag: one pink and one yellow. Both mine.

Then I ran.

Peter scrambled to his feet and chased after me, leaving Jessie swinging around behind us.

With Peter's breath hot on my neck, I launched myself at the first palm tree I saw and scrambled up till I was fifteen feet in the air. Clutching the trunk, I glanced down. Peter stood at the base of the tree, huffing with exhaustion.

"Coward!" he yelled. "Come down here!"

From up here, I had a new chance to get

away. To my right was a large tree with wide, thick branches that could support me. The idea came to me in a flash. *I can go from tree to tree until the end of the challenge . . . or at least until Peter gives up.* Being stuck in the treetops for the rest of the day didn't sound exciting, but it was the only way.

I was about to make my move when Peter seemed to get an idea. He went over to the tree I was about to jump to and began to climb. He hoisted himself up clumsily to the lowest branches. Once he found his balance, he grabbed the next branch. He was coming up after me.

What am I going to do? I thought, panicking. I looked to my left. There was nothing within my reach but a couple of thin, weak branches and big leaves. I hugged the trunk tighter. Peter was almost at my height now. Soon, he'd shuffle out and grab the flags off my hip while I stayed stuck in the tree. Like a coward.

Unless . . .

Right as Peter swiped at me, I loosened my grip and slid back down the trunk of the palm tree. The friction burned my fingers, but I was on the ground in seconds.

I took off into the forest, leaving him and Jessie behind.

I spent the rest of the first round hiding as best I could. I heard Jessie and Peter complaining in the distance as they searched for me. Every time they got close, I flattened myself to the forest floor and slowed my breathing. They passed right by me. My experiences watching wild animals were coming in handy. I snuck back to my camp after dark and let the shadows of the overhang protect me from any prying eyes.

As the first round neared completion, my emotions soared. I thought about my parents back home. It filled me with more energy than food ever could.

At sunrise the next morning, a series of three huge booms filled the island air, jolting me awake and signaling the end of the first round.

"Competitors, please make your way east!" Chase's voice called from hidden speakers.

The dawn of this new day meant the beginning of the second round. And I had gotten enough flags to move on.

CHAPTER 5

Chase stood in his large, white boat. I stood in the sand along with the other competitors. I held the yellow and pink flags in my hands. In my pockets were the canteen and the pig statue.

Chase jumped down from the boat and waded over to us. A cameraman followed him, sticking his camera in each of our faces. It felt weird to be able to see the camera up close like this. I frowned when it was my turn to get examined.

"Jessie, Peter, Ramon, Kyle, Isabel," Chase said when he reached the end of the line. "As you were not able to keep any flags, your time on *Teen Wilderness Masters* has come to an end. Please board the boat to return home."

The five competitors waded back to the boat hanging their heads. Jessie and Peter gave me one last annoyed look. I smiled back at them.

Then I turned to evaluate who was left. Next to me was the muscly guy I ran into first. He winked at me. But I could tell by the sneer on his face that he was trying to intimidate me. I frowned and looked past him at the others: the stocky, grim-looking girl I sat next to on the boat; a skinny kid who was picking his teeth; and finally, Amanda, who stared straight ahead.

"The rest of you—Ethan, Richie, Diana, Travis, and Amanda—congratulations! You are on your way to becoming the next Teen Wilderness Master." Chase grinned broadly. He named us in the order we were standing in—that meant Mr. Muscles was Richie, the grumpy girl was Diana, and the skinny boy was Travis.

"Now, hand in your flags. We will no longer be needing them."

After we handed over our flags, Chase explained the next round. We would join together to survive as a group. There would be six challenges, where we would all compete against one another for a reward. The reward for three of the challenges was a delicious meal. The reward for the other three was immunity from one elimination.

"Since there are three immunity challenges, there will be three elimination sessions," Chase continued. "Which means three of you will not make it to the final round of *Teen Wilderness Masters*. And the best part? You'll get to vote on who to eliminate!" Chase looked intensely at each of us. "So . . . think you have what it takes to make it to the final round?"

The others nodded. *Absolutely*, I thought, nodding too. My competitors might have been good at making traps or had big muscles, but I was smart and fast—*and* motivated by my family. I just hoped my survival skills would be enough.

Before he sent us off, Chase gave us some essential supplies: more flint, two machetes for chopping down trees and opening coconuts, and a starter pack of rice and beans. "Your first challenge will take place tomorrow, so I suggest you get to work on a shelter," he concluded. Then he returned to the boat, leaving us alone on the island once again.

As soon as the boat was gone, Richie knelt down and unpacked the supplies.

"I'll take this," he said, picking up one of the machetes. He looked up at the other girl. "Diana, right? You get the other one. Travis, you can carry the flint, and Amanda—"

I frowned. "Shouldn't we decide things as a group?"

"What's wrong with Diana having the other machete?" he asked in an accusing tone.

"Nothing, but—"

"I think it's better for me and her to start out with them," he interrupted. "No offense, but we're clearly the strongest. We'll cut down the trees, and the rest of you can help put them together for our shelter."

Richie had a point, but I didn't like how he didn't let the rest of us weigh in. But I decided it wasn't worth arguing over. *I need to stay on everyone's good side for now.* This second round was about teamwork and alliances. We were competitors in challenges against one another, but how we behaved outside of the challenges mattered too.

Richie stood up. "Come on, everyone. Follow me," he said, grinning widely as if he could convince me he was friendly.

I started after him, and then the others followed me. We headed into the jungle to look for fallen trees that we could use as building materials.

As we walked, Richie said that we should build our shelter on the southern beach. The ocean there was calm and full of fish.

"There's a cliff in the jungle we could take shelter under," I suggested. "It's right next to a stream with fresh water. If we go there, we don't have to build as much. All it needs is some reinforcement."

"That's a good point," Amanda said.

"Well, I think Richie's on the right track. I also want to go to the beach," Travis piped up.

Richie stopped walking and turned to face the rest of us, hands on his hips. "Let's take a vote."

The vote was three to two, with Diana deciding to vote for the beach. So we went south, even though I thought it was much smarter to build in the jungle. I felt more at home in there, among the animals and the trees. But I was also realizing it was easier to let Richie have his way.

When we reached the spot where Richie wanted to build, he turned around and pointed at each of us. "You, Diana. Got your machete? Good. Let's go chop down some trees. Travis, Ethan, and Amanda? You'll be in charge of putting the shelter together."

I didn't argue this time.

Richie went off into the woods, with Diana on his heels. Amanda, Travis, and I set out to collect fallen palm leaves and sticks we could use for the shelter. While Amanda went off on her own, I talked with Travis. It turned out he was a skilled fisherman. He had grown up on boats in the Atlantic Ocean and could reel in a full-grown tuna on his own. He wanted to win *Teen Wilderness Masters* to buy his own boat and go sailing around the world.

After Diana and Richie returned with some skinny trees they had chopped down, we built walls for our shelter. Amanda weaved together palm tree leaves to make a roof.

"Let me make something clear to everyone right now," she said as she worked. "I don't want any food from the storage boxes or from Chase. None of those rice and beans." She picked up another leaf from the pile next to her. "I'll feed myself."

Richie shrugged. "All right."

"But I also won't be sharing any food I find with the rest of you. Instead, if you want something I've got, you'll have to make a trade for it."

"Whoa, wait a second. We're supposed to share things," Travis said. "That's the point of this part of the game. To work together."

"Trading is like sharing," Amanda said.

"Let's vote on it," Richie said. Voting seemed to be his favorite way to make decisions. "If you want to trade things, raise your hand."

Amanda raised hers. Then she looked at me. I swallowed, feeling guilty for not voting along with her. I hoped she understood that my vote had nothing to do with me siding against her. It was smarter to share everything. Well—not everything. I would keep the pig figurine a secret for the time being.

"Four to one," Richie said.

Amanda sighed, "Fine. I'll share what I collect with the group. But I still don't want any of the stuff that the show gives to us."

After that, it became even clearer that none of the others liked Amanda. I seemed to be the only one who wanted to talk to her. I told her about how I tricked Peter and Jessie, then she taught me how to weave palm leaves. We worked on the roof together.

Richie kept ordering everyone around, and with every barked command, I felt my shoulders tense up. I wanted to win this because of my own actions, not by what someone else told me to do. After we finished the shelter, he assigned me to the task of shoveling out a toilet for us. When I said it was smarter to just go in the ocean, he told me it wasn't nice of me to be lazy. "Look at everyone else doing their fair share," he said. Diana and Travis nodded in agreement with Richie, so I did what Richie told me to do.

When Richie went off into the jungle to get some more materials, I tried to bond with Travis and Diana about how bossy he was.

"Oh, he's bossy all right," Diana said. "But he's also strong and a good planner. So I think he's worth keeping around. Unlike her." She jabbed a thumb at Amanda, who sat away from us, tending to the fire.

"She's skilled too," I protested. "She's really good at living off the land. She even caught me in a trap and took my flag during the first round."

"She took your flag?" Diana scoffed. "Man, you must have gotten lucky to make it to the second round."

Travis laughed while I blushed.

I went to bed that first night feeling lousy. This was a competition, sure, but couldn't it be a friendly competition? I closed my eyes and drifted to sleep.

CHAPTER 6

"Rise and shine!" Chase's voice cried.

Coming out of sleep, I squinted against the sunlight. Chase had showed up on the beach right outside our shelter.

"You all ready for the first reward challenge?" He grinned as we got to our feet.

After we ate breakfast, we boarded the boat and looped around the island to the eastern shore. The water was choppy, making the boat bounce and jerk. Richie looked like he was going to be ill. Diana actually *was* ill. *There goes her share of the rice and beans.*

The wind was even stronger on the

beach. It felt like it was blowing from every direction.

We walked inland until we reached a small field surrounded by trees. Dangling up high in the trees were ceramic targets of different colors: red, orange, yellow, green, and blue. And cameras. Lots of cameras. The targets swayed in the wind.

Chase led us to the edge of the field, where five slingshots rested on a wooden table. In front of the table was a basket full of pebbles. From here, I could see three white lines painted on the ground in the field: one about five yards away from us, another at fifteen yards, and another at thirty.

"Welcome to the first challenge of the second round of *Teen Wilderness Masters*," Chase said in a dramatic voice. "It's time to show us your marksmanship skills. In this challenge, each of you will use a slingshot to shoot the stones in this basket at the targets hanging around the field. Each target you break is worth one point."

Seems simple enough, I thought.

"You have to shoot from behind the white lines to avoid hitting each other. Once you break your first target, you can go up to the second line, and so on," Chase continued. "But make sure you match the color of the slingshot's handle to the color of the targets. If you break someone else's target, it counts toward their score, not yours! The first person to score three points wins."

My fingers twitched in anticipation. I used to play with slingshots a lot as a kid. I only shot at objects, like cans or pinecones, but I got pretty good at aiming.

"I'm sure you're all still pretty hungry," Chase said, winking at the camera. "The winner of this challenge will be rewarded with a huge breakfast. Plus, a surprise."

Although I wondered what the surprise could be, I really wanted that food. Even though we'd just eaten, I was still so hungry after hardly having anything to eat these past few days. I glanced down the line at my competition. They all seemed equally eager to get started.

Chase grinned as a gust of wind blew through the playing field. "Good luck, everyone!"

I picked up the slingshot closest to me, the red one, and then grabbed a fistful of the pebbles. I shoved the pebbles into my pocket and headed out to the first painted line. My red target hung from one of the highest branches. Amanda came up beside me, holding the green slingshot. In one quick motion, like a cowboy in a duel, she aimed and fired the pebble at her target. *Crack!* The target split into two pieces with the sound of a dinner plate breaking.

"Amazing! Amanda has scored the first point of the game!" Chase announced.

Amazing was right. Amanda raced forward to the second line while the rest of us were stunned. Then I shot off my own first stone, which missed by a mile.

By the time I hit my first target, I was in third place—behind Amanda and Richie.

I sprinted to the second line and skidded to a stop next to Richie. My second target was even higher, which meant it was exposed to more wind. Every time my rocks seemed to be getting close to it, the wind blew the target in the opposite direction.

"Oh, come on!" I heard Richie mutter on my left. *At least I'm not the only one having trouble.*

Amanda was to my right, quiet and concentrating hard. She had her slingshot drawn and was taking her time to aim. She hadn't fired a second shot at all yet.

Then, she released. Bull's-eye.

I squinted at my target as it swung back and forth. If I could time my shot right, then the target would swing into the pebble. I drew back and waited, like Amanda, for the perfect shot. Next to me, Richie kept shooting away. Diana scored a point and joined us at the second line. Travis was still stuck trying to hit his first one.

Now! I released. The pebble soared and struck my target.

"Two points to Ethan!" Chase announced.

Richie glared at me as I joined Amanda at the final target.

She stood calmly, waiting again for the right moment. If I didn't act fast, I was going to lose to her. I reached into my pocket and realized with horror that I was out of pebbles. I'd have to run back to the basket and grab some more. I turned on my heel, ready to race back to the table when—*crack!*

Too late. The final green target broke.

"Amanda is our winner!" Chase cried.

I slinked back to the starting point to drop off my slingshot. Even if I'd had a pebble in my pocket, I probably didn't stand a chance against Amanda. But I was still upset. I really wanted that reward.

"Congratulations, Amanda," Chase said when we had all returned to the table. "You've won a breakfast buffet."

I clapped for her, and so did Diana and Travis. Reluctantly, Richie joined in.

"Now, to reveal the surprise."

Oh yeah. I'd forgotten about that.

"I hope you've made a friend because one of your fellow competitors will be allowed to join you for breakfast. You get to choose!"

I perked up at that. There was only one person in the group who had any sort of closeness to her, and that person was . . . "I pick Ethan," Amanda said, without any hesitation.

***

Chase took Amanda and me by boat to another tiny, deserted island. On the beach, there was a table covered with pastries, omelets, and fresh fruit. The table had a tablecloth, and there were plates and utensils. For a moment, I felt like I wasn't on a reality TV show but instead at a fancy tropical restaurant.

Chase told us we couldn't take any of the food back with us, so I ate as much as possible. I shoveled scrambled eggs into my mouth and washed it down with fresh orange juice. The strawberries were much better than the wild berries I ate with the pig.

As I ate, Amanda sat there in silence. She kept her hands in her lap.

"Aren't you going to have any?" I asked through a mouthful of croissant.

"No. I didn't find it myself."

"But you won it yourself."

She sighed. "This meal would never appear in the wild."

"Neither would that competition," I pointed out. "So you might as well eat up. It'll give us an advantage in the next challenge."

"I'd rather win using the skills I already have," she said stubbornly. "I want to do everything without any special assistance."

I frowned and went back to eating. Amanda was too headstrong. She wasn't eating any of the food she needed to regain her strength. She didn't want to make friends with the others. I agreed that the competition was mostly about skill. But "skill" included teamwork and knowing when to accept help. If she didn't win the immunity challenge tomorrow, the others would probably vote her off. And, so far, she was the only one who was nice to me. I didn't want her to go just yet.

***

When Amanda and I walked back into camp, Richie, Travis, and Diana were all sitting around the fire, whispering. They immediately stopped talking when we got there, and they didn't respond when I waved at them. I let my hand drop down. *I guess they're still upset that Amanda picked me.*

That evening, Travis and Richie cooked a fish they caught and shared it with Diana. But not me and Amanda. "It's only fair," explained Richie. "You two got food that we didn't get to eat, so now we have food that you don't get to eat."

"It's not our fault you didn't get any of the breakfast," I said.

"Well, we caught this fish," Richie said.

I looked to Amanda for help, but she just shrugged.

We tried to catch our own fish but had no luck. So I was stuck with rice and beans again, and Amanda ate some berries she'd found.

Now I kind of wished Amanda hadn't chosen me. Or hadn't been allowed to choose anyone at all. Because while we were out enjoying our reward, our three competitors had a whole morning to strategize against us.

To form an alliance.

And nothing was tougher to beat than an alliance.

CHAPTER 7

The next challenge took place the following day. Chase brought us to the island where Amanda and I had eaten the reward breakfast. In high tide, the tiny island became two, with a mile-wide channel of water in between them. We jumped from the boat to the white sand beach on the western island.

Lined up in a row on the sand were five colored mats. In the middle of the channel of water, far from us, were five colored poles to match. I squinted to get a better view and thought I saw something shining in the sunlight on top of the poles.

Chase directed each of us to a mat. I chose the red one again.

For a moment I felt like I was at a summer camp, about to begin an interesting scavenger hunt. But the illusion was broken by the camera crew, complete with fuzzy microphones and huge headphones, who set up their equipment all over the beach.

"Today's challenge is a race," Chase began. "Beginning on the beach here, you will swim out to the poles in the water. Once you're at your pole, dive down to untie a key from the bottom. Then, climb the pole to the top and use your key to unlock the treasure chest there. Swim back to shore carrying the item from the chest to the mats here on the beach. The first person to return to the start with their item wins the challenge."

This sounded like an intense test of physical ability. *Normally, I could climb that pole*, I thought. *But can I do it after swimming for half a mile on a mostly empty stomach?*

"The reward for this challenge is immunity," Chase continued. "That means that during the first voting session tonight, no one can vote for the winner. Sound good to everyone?"

We all nodded.

"On my count—!" Chase raised his hands into the air. "Are you ready? Three! Two! One! Go!"

I launched off my mat and sprinted to the blue-green water. I took a couple steps into the waves and dove in. I swam with everything I had. My muscles began to ache quickly. But the food I had eaten yesterday powered me out farther and farther from the shore. I tasted salt as water splashed across my face.

I got to the red pole faster than I expected, and suddenly it was in front of me. I stopped swimming and bobbed up and down for a moment, shaking the water from my face. Next to me, I saw bubbles at the orange pole, meaning Richie was already here. He was underwater, looking for his key.

I have to beat Richie. It was the only way to prevent his alliance from voting me off tonight.

I dove down, keeping my eyes open.

The salt stung and made everything blurry. Thankfully, the water was only about ten feet deep. The key was attached to a cord wrapped around the base of the pole. I grabbed it and started working on the knot to free it.

When my lungs started burning even more than my eyes, I shot back up to the surface and caught my breath. Diana and Travis had arrived at their poles now. Amanda was still swimming over, slowly but surely.

I freed my key on the second dive. Next came climbing the pole. It was slippery with my wet hands and feet. I put the key between my teeth and shimmied up like a wet cat with no claws. For every foot I gained I slid down six inches. On the orange pole, Richie had opened his treasure chest and dropped into the water to swim back.

I scrambled up the rest of the pole and plunged my key into the treasure chest. The lid popped open, revealing . . . a rock.

A big, round, heavy rock.

Oh, Chase is evil.

I scooped up the rock and fell back into the

water with a huge splash. I nearly dropped the rock, which would have been awful because then I'd have to dive for it. Already exhausted, I groaned out loud and started doggy-paddling my way back to shore, one arm doing all the swimming and the other clutching the rock.

I passed Amanda, who still hadn't reached her pole. She looked exhausted and weak, and I realized she was struggling to swim.

But I couldn't stop and worry about her now. I had to beat Richie. He was only a few yards ahead of me.

I swam with all my strength. Even though the rock weighed me down, I imagined myself cutting through the water like a fish. *You got this, Ethan. You can do—*

Wham!

My knees crashed into the shore a lot quicker than expected. The rock slipped out of my hands as I tried to stand up. Waves splashed into my legs, nearly knocking me over. I grabbed the rock again and ran back to my mat.

"Ethan," Chase's voice said from above me.

"You've won the first immunity challenge!"

"Wait, I did?" I looked over my shoulder. Diana and Travis were swimming back from their poles. Amanda was hanging on to hers, too tired to continue. Standing in the shallow water, his mouth open in disbelief, was Richie. He let his own rock fall with a huge splash.

I laughed out of relief and exhaustion. Chase handed me a thick wooden stick that had been carved with patterns and symbols. "This stick represents immunity," he said.

I smiled weakly, too exhausted to celebrate.

CHAPTER 8

Back at camp, the power trio of Richie, Diana, and Travis marched off into the woods to strategize. I didn't really know what they had to strategize about—obviously, they'd be voting for Amanda tonight.

I sat down at the fire next to Amanda. I held the immunity stick out in front of me, tracing the carvings with my fingers. "Are you okay? You didn't look very happy during the challenge."

"I was too weak," she sighed. "Climbing up that pole would have been impossible. When I saw you and Richie racing back to shore, I just gave up. There was no way I'd catch up to you. And now I'm going home."

"Hey, you still have a chance. We can convince either Travis or Diana to vote for Richie with us."

Amanda just rolled her eyes. "Get real, Ethan. I know they don't like me."

"You can make a trade with them," I suggested.

"A trade?"

I explained my idea to her.

Her eyes brightened. "It's worth a shot," she said.

When the others returned, Travis left to check the fish snares. Richie started a pot of rice. Diana walked down to the shore, away from everyone else.

I went to Travis first to explain my plan to him. But before I could finish making my offer, he scoffed and waved me off. "Yeah, right! Sorry, dude, but I'm voting for Amanda. She's gotta go."

Fine. I didn't expect him to agree, anyway. I left him and sauntered up to Diana. She was drawing a picture of an island in the wet sand. With a flick of her wrist, she used the sand to add texture and depth to the picture. I squatted beside her.

"You're a good artist," I remarked after a little while.

"Thanks." She put down her stick. "I know why you're here, Ethan. You want me to vote with you and Amanda."

"Guilty as charged," I shrugged. "We wanted to make a deal with you."

"Well, I'll hear you out. If your deal is better than the one Richie just made with me, I'll agree to it."

"What did Richie offer you?"

Diana smirked. "It's a secret."

I looked out across the water. Some clouds were coming in to shore. "In exchange for you agreeing to vote for Richie tonight, Amanda and I promise to let you win the next reward challenge. We'll throw it for you. All you'd have to do is beat Travis, but since he likes you, maybe you can convince him to let you win too."

"Hmm." She tapped the stick in the sand, thinking it over. "That's a pretty good deal, I have to admit."

"Will you do it?"

"You'll find out tonight." She winked.

***

The sunset lit up the clouds bright pink. In the distance, Chase's boat zoomed toward the beach. I sat next to Amanda and trembled with nerves. I hoped Diana would take our offer and help us get rid of Richie.

When Chase arrived, the five of us gathered around our campfire and listened as he introduced the rules of the voting session. One by one, we would climb aboard his boat. In the cabin of the boat was a panel of five colored buttons, one for each of us. All we had to do was push the button for the person we wanted to vote for. After everyone voted, we'd find out who was going home.

"But there's one more trick to this." Chase narrowed his eyes, looking mysterious in the fire's light, like he was telling a ghost story.

"In addition to having the immunity stick, there is one more way to avoid getting voted off. Hidden on the island in a supply box was a secret immunity talisman, and one of you found it. It looks like this."

He reached into his jacket and pulled out a small, wooden sculpture of a pig. It was identical to the one in my own pocket.

"After everyone casts their vote, I will ask if someone wants to use the immunity talisman," Chase went on. "If someone decides to play the talisman, all the votes made against them will be discarded."

I swallowed. I could give the talisman to Amanda right now. *But it came from a supply box—what if she doesn't want it?* If she said no, then everyone else would know I had it. If she took it, and I didn't win any of the immunity challenges afterward, I'd be voted off in a second. *Do I keep it for myself or help Amanda out?*

"Let's proceed with the vote," Chase said, interrupting my thoughts. "Richie, you're up first."

One by one, each of us vanished into the boat. The panel had five buttons on it: red for me, orange for Richie, yellow for Diana, green for Amanda, and blue for Travis. Since I had the immunity stick, the red button wasn't lit up, but the others were. I pushed the orange button.

After everyone had voted, Chase tallied the votes. When he returned to the beach, he asked, "Would anyone like to play the secret immunity talisman now?"

I didn't move. I had to hold on to the hope that Diana would vote with us. *I'm sorry, Amanda. Please understand.*

"Very well. Then the first person voted off of *Teen Wilderness Masters* is . . ."

I looked at Richie. If he was about to go home, I wanted to see that smug grin wiped off his face.

My heart pounded in my ears.

The ocean crashed against the shore.

The boat suddenly lit up green.

"Amanda!"

No! I glared at Diana, but she was staring

in awe at the boat. I wondered what Richie had offered her that was better than the promise of winning the next challenge.

"Amanda, please follow me." Chase gestured at her. She obeyed and soon disappeared onto the boat that still shone her color.

CHAPTER 9

I woke up with a headache the next day. The sunlight hurt my eyes. I wished it would rain so I could lie down on the sand and let it soak me. I still couldn't believe Amanda had been voted off.

But it was time for the next challenge. "Come on, lazy," Richie said to me. He, Travis, and Diana were all ready to go. I groaned and got to my feet.

Chase picked us up from the beach and took us back to the field on the other side of the island. He collected the immunity stick from me and then explained the challenge.

Lined up in the field were four tile puzzles.

We had to slide the tiles around in each of our puzzles to create a picture. But each of the fifteen tiles could only move one space at a time, and only one tile could move at a time. I had played puzzles like this before, but I was never very good at them. The only thing I knew to do was put the corners and edges in place first, then try to arrange the middle tiles.

The reward was a huge picnic buffet. As with the first challenge, the winner would be allowed to invite someone else to join them.

Chase raised his hand to signal the start of the challenge. I stared at the colors on the wooden board and slid the tiles around aimlessly. My head pounded, and I couldn't think straight. I had about six tiles in place when Richie cried, "Got it!"

Chase went over to the orange board. He studied Richie's creation for a while and then said, "Richie is our winner!"

If Diana had taken my offer, that could have been her, I thought bitterly. I crossed my arms as Richie said he wanted Diana to join him for the meal. *I bet that's what Richie offered her.*

Travis and I had to march back to the camp on foot. I knew I needed a new ally, so along the way, I decided to see what he would be open to.

"Have you seen the wild pigs on the island?" I asked. "They're pretty cute."

"No." Travis shook his head. "I spent most of the first round on the beach. So I mostly saw fish and seagulls."

"How'd you get your second flag, then?"

"I found a supply box hidden in some driftwood. I took what I wanted from it, and then closed it back up and left it where I found it. Then I just waited. After a while, someone else came along, and when he was bent over, looking at the box, I snuck up and grabbed his flag." For a moment, Travis looked proud. "He didn't even notice until I was gone."

"Sneaky!" I said. "So . . . you think you have a chance at winning the game?"

"Of course I do. I wouldn't be here if I didn't."

"You think Richie's going to take you to the end?"

Travis just scoffed. "It's going to be the other way around. Richie couldn't last without me."

"You sure about that? You haven't won any of the challenges yet. And Richie picked Diana to go with him to the reward."

Travis didn't reply. I noticed that his footsteps turned to stomps. *Good.*

"You and I could work together," I said. "I have a trick up my sleeve that Richie will never see coming." Well, in my pocket.

"Sure you do, Ethan." He rolled his eyes.

"I think Richie and Diana are going to vote you off as soon as I'm gone. But, if you join me, we have a chance to take them out."

"Nice try, dude. But I'm going to win the immunity challenge tomorrow, and the immunity challenge after that. I don't need your help."

With that, Travis sped up, his feet crushing dead leaves and branches. I let out a huge sigh and trudged after him.

Back at the camp, Travis announced he was going fishing.

"Can I come?" I asked.

"No way," Travis said. "You'll just get in my way. Leave the fishing to the expert."

He sharpened a stick to make a fishing spear and then headed west along the beach. Once he was out of sight, I followed his footprints in the sand.

After a short walk, we reached a wall of rocks, moss, and vines. Travis lifted himself up the rocks and disappeared over the top. As quietly as possible, I climbed up after him and peeked out over the ledge. On the other side of the wall was a lagoon full of sparkling green water and fish. Travis stood in the shallow water near the shore, looking for the perfect fish to catch. He was concentrating hard and didn't seem to notice me at all—which was just fine with me. If he wouldn't let me join him, then maybe I could learn something from him in secret.

Soon enough, a large shadow appeared in the water. A big fish. Travis reached into his pocket and took out a handful of dry rice. He sprinkled it into the water in front of him.

The big shadow swam a little closer to him and nibbled at the rice.

Travis hurled the spear at it.

With a huge splash, the fish darted away and disappeared. Travis growled in frustration.

I snuck back to camp and grabbed my own fistful of rice. I jammed it into my pocket right as Travis returned moments later, without any fish.

"No luck?" I asked.

He grumbled in response. He threw aside his spear and went into the shelter. "Going to nap."

Perfect. As soon as he started snoring, I grabbed his spear and went back to the lagoon.

The water was warm in the sunlight. Small, colorful fish circled my feet. My headache faded the longer I stood there. After a short while, I spied a dark spot coming close to me. I took out some of the rice from my pocket and sprinkled it into the water in front of me, just like Travis had done.

The dark spot inched closer. I jabbed my spear with all my might at the shadow and lifted a fish into the air. *Got it!*

I carried my catch back to the camp. Travis had woken up and was tending to the fire. He stared at me in disbelief when he saw that I'd caught a fish.

"Want to team up with me now?" I asked him, placing the fish on a large piece of tree bark.

He crossed his arms and huffed. I hoped he could see now that I was a valuable competitor and, more importantly, a good ally.

A short while later, Richie and Diana returned from their reward meal. They stumbled back into camp beaming.

Travis rushed up to greet them. "Welcome back," he said immediately. "For when you two get hungry again, I've got some fish here for you."

"Whoa, nice catch!" Richie exclaimed, seeing the size of the fish. "Great work, Travis."

"Oh, that was me," I said. "I caught it."

They all stared at me.

Then Travis let out a short laugh. "You're

joking, right? Everyone knows I'm the best fisherman here. I obviously caught the fish."

My mouth opened in disbelief. "You saw me bring it back to camp."

"Quit lying, Ethan," Travis sneered. "It's embarrassing."

Richie and Diana started laughing.

"I'm not lying," I protested, feeling my face heat up. "I caught that fish while Travis slept in the shelter." He pointed to the spear Travis made. "There's the spear I used."

"You mean, the spear I used," Travis said.

All three of them kept laughing. Richie and Diana were never going to believe that I had caught it. *Why is Travis doing this to me?* I wondered. *I haven't done anything to him.*

The three of them sat down in the shelter, leaving me standing alone on the sand. Travis and Diana kept talking at the same time, each trying to get Richie's attention. As I watched them, suddenly everything made sense. Diana and Travis were jealous of each other. Travis knew Richie liked Diana better, so he lied about catching the fish in order to impress

Richie. And Diana seemed to be willing to jump through hoops just to stay on Richie's good side. In their minds, I was going to be the next one to go home. They were planning ahead, trying to secure their spot in the final two by appealing to Richie.

But they didn't know I had the secret immunity talisman.

CHAPTER 10

The next immunity challenge was a wrestling match: a test of physical strength. We drew straws to determine the matchups: Diana would face Richie, and I would square off against Travis. The winners of those two matches would then compete against each other. To win each match, you had to either pin your opponent down for ten seconds straight or push them out of the ring.

Diana and Richie went first. I crossed my fingers, hoping Diana would win. But Richie was too heavy for her to move, and inch by inch she was backed into a corner. Finally, she was forced out of the ring.

Then it was my turn against Travis. He was taller than I was, but my anger from the day before motivated me. The second that Chase told us to start, I charged at him. I grabbed him around the waist and yanked him to the ground. Surprised at my own strength, I held him firmly in place.

While Travis flailed underneath me, Chase counted to ten. “And Ethan defeats Travis!” he called.

Too exhausted to do anything else, Travis just glared at me as he joined Diana on the sideline.

“And now, for the final round,” Chase said dramatically for the cameras, “we have . . . Ethan versus Richie!”

Crap.

Richie entered the ring, cracked his knuckles, and sneered down at me. I gulped.

“Start!” Chase yelled.

At once, Richie rushed me. I tried to dodge so he’d accidentally step outside, but he was too fast. He whirled around and grabbed my waist, then lifted me into the air. I cried out, surprised at how easily he lifted me. It was like being caught in Amanda's trap.

Richie plopped me down on the sand, outside of the ring. Then he raised his fists into the air in triumph—he had won the challenge. Chase handed him the immunity stick. And that meant I couldn't vote for him tonight.

I had to choose between Diana and Travis. Diana had voted for Amanda, so I was tempted to vote for her. But Travis had lied about catching the fish and humiliated me, and I didn't want to keep him around for much longer either.

That evening, Chase came to our campsite and began the voting session.

"You have all come a long way and shown impressive wilderness skills," he said. "But for one of you, the journey comes to an end tonight. Let's vote."

I went first. On the boat, staring down at the glowing buttons, my finger hovered between yellow for Diana and blue for Travis. I made my choice without hesitation.

After we all submitted our votes, Chase returned. "Now," he said, "would anyone like to play the immunity talisman?"

The fire crackled. Richie glanced around, turning the immunity stick over and over in his hands as if to show it off. Travis and Diana looked at each other. None of them suspected me. When I stood up and pulled the pig statue out of my pocket, their jaws dropped.

"Ethan plays the immunity talisman!" Chase announced. "That means all votes cast against him are invalid. As it so happens, that means three of the four votes have been discarded." Chase grinned mischievously. "The next person voted off of *Teen Wilderness Masters* is . . ."

The boat burst into blue light.

"Travis!"

Travis shot me an angry look before he stood up to leave. Richie and Diana were still dumbstruck. Travis boarded the boat, and then it was just the three of us.

CHAPTER 11

At the final reward challenge, Chase gave the three of us a choice. "We can go ahead with the reward challenge as planned," he said, "where one of you wins a fabulous meal. Or, if the three of you agree, we can skip the challenge and give everyone something to eat."

Whoa, I thought. *That would be awesome.*

"But," Chase continued, "all three of you have to agree to skip the reward challenge. If even one of you votes against it, then you will all have to do the challenge."

"Well, I vote for the food," I said.

"Me too," Richie said.

Diana furrowed her brow.

"Come on, Diana. If you vote with us, you're guaranteed something to eat. If you vote against us, you could lose the challenge and not get anything," Richie pointed out. "Do you *really* wanna risk that?"

She sighed. "Okay, fine. Let's share it."

Chase clapped his hands and grinned. "Excellent! I was hoping you three would choose that."

At Chase's signal, some crew members wheeled out a table with three platters covered by silver lids. Then they brought out three chairs and asked us to take a seat. I sat in the middle chair and looked at the platter, imagining what kind of delicious meal awaited me. My stomach growled. I reached to lift up the cover.

"Hold on a second, Ethan. There's one more thing I have to go over," Chase said.

I squinted at him, confused.

"Since the three of you have elected to skip the reward challenge, we will move right into the immunity challenge." Chase broke into a mischievous grin that made my stomach drop. "The challenge is simple enough. The first person to eat everything on their plate wins immunity. Sound good?"

The three of us glanced at each other, and my stomach dropped. *Something's up.*

"Go ahead and dig in!"

I lifted the lid off my plate and tossed it aside. My excitement at getting to eat immediately turned to confusion and horror. Peering up at me from my plate were three cooked crickets. Huge, spiny, buggy *crickets.*

Next to me, Diana gagged. She had a pair of juicy cockroaches on her platter. On my other side, Richie was silent, staring at the tarantula curled up in front of him.

"Enjoy," Chase said, practically laughing.

I gulped, but my throat was dry. I knew that in some places in the world, people ate bugs like it was no big deal. As a small child, I even tried a couple ants. But these crickets were each as long as my thumb—and about as fat too. I picked one up by its long back leg.

Suddenly, Richie burst into a coughing fit.

I glanced over and saw him spit out one of the tarantula's legs. A shudder ran through me.

"Anyone need some salt and pepper?" Chase asked mockingly.

"Actually," I said, "I could do with some." Even if I was totally disgusted, I could pretend that I wasn't and psyche Richie and Diana out.

Chase's grin widened as he brought containers of each to me.

I salted and peppered my crickets. Diana and Richie watched in horror as I lifted one to my lips and took a huge bite. The crunch echoed in my head. One of the legs stuck to my chin. I chewed, grimacing. It tasted a little bit like potato chips or sunflower seeds. Like a nut. I closed my eyes and pretended it was anything besides a cricket. *A pretzel*, I told myself. *It's just a crunchy pretzel.* When I swallowed, the spines on the legs scratched my throat.

I braced myself and finished the first cricket. *Only two to go.*

Diana hadn't even touched her bugs. She poked at one of the cockroaches and covered her mouth, looking ill. Richie stared down at his tarantula, picking spider hairs off his tongue. I ate my second cricket.

The third was the easiest to eat and swallow. Chase came over and inspected my plate, then had me open my mouth to prove I had swallowed everything.

"We have our winner!" he declared, handing me the immunity stick. "With this win, Ethan gains a special privilege. Since Richie and Diana must vote for each other, their votes cancel out. So his vote is the only one that matters tonight. Ethan, I hope you make your decision wisely."

I swallowed again, this time out of nervousness.

CHAPTER 12

Back at camp, I told Diana and Richie that I would talk to each of them separately in order to decide who I wanted to vote for. They were both very skilled competitors, and neither of them was my friend. Even though I didn't like Richie very much, Diana could be tough to beat in the end too, depending on what the final round was. I had to play smart, and that meant weighing my options.

I spoke to Diana first. We walked to the shore and sat down in the sand. She nervously shoved her hands into the sand. I took a deep breath and asked her why she wanted to win.

"I'm here to prove myself to my family," she said. "Do you know who Paolo Gonzales is?"

I nodded.

"Well, he's my father."

I gasped in surprise. Paolo Gonzales was one of the most famous contestants in the history of *Wilderness Masters*. He had been on the show three times, and he won twice. He used the prize money to create a summer camp for young nature-lovers, to train them in the art of survival and self-reliance. Diana must have grown up in that camp.

"It's in my blood to win," she said fiercely. "And once I do, I'm going to put my money toward art school. My dream is to be a famous artist—someday I'll be even more famous than my dad." She glowed with pride.

"How come your dad doesn't help out with that?" I asked, confused. "He's made a lot of money winning *Wilderness Masters*, right?"

Diana's smile faded. "He isn't too happy about me wanting to be an artist. He wants me to follow in his footsteps. That's why I have to do this on my own." She took a deep breath.

"Everyone back home is rooting for me. I'm the daughter of Paolo Gonzales. I can't lose."

"It sounds like you're under a lot of pressure."

"It isn't pressure," she scoffed. "It's my birthright. It would be an honor to lose to me!"

I snorted. *She can't be serious.* But as I glanced at her again, I could see her doubt. She picked up a stick and furiously scribbled in the sand.

I left her to continue doodling in the sand and returned to the campsite, where I sat at the fire by Richie. He was cooking up some dinner for the three of us.

"What's up?" he grunted, not even looking up at me.

"I think you know what's up."

"My turn to convince you to keep me around?" He tossed some extra sticks on the fire. "I thought you'd want me gone. I've been nothing but a jerk to you this whole time."

Whatever I had expected him to say, it wasn't that. *So he knows how mean he was?* I studied his face, trying to understand what he meant. “Why were you a jerk to me then?” I asked.

“Because I was scared of you,” he said, his eyes still on the fire. “You outmatched me and everyone else from the beginning. In the first round, you stole not just one, but *two* flags from other players. You befriended Amanda when no one else could. You almost won the first challenge. And then you won the second challenge. You even had the immunity talisman this whole time! This whole game seems to come to you so easily.” Richie paused and said quietly, “I don’t stand a chance against you.”

I raised my eyebrows. “Wow. Well, thanks. I think you’re also a good competitor, though. I’m not perfect.”

“No, but if you take me to the final round, you’ll definitely win.” Richie finally made eye contact with me. “Which kind of sucks because I really wanted the prize money. I was going to donate it to a conservation organization in Africa.”

I blinked at him. “Really?”

"Mhmm." He nodded. "They're working on saving the endangered animals there. But you're a good person who cares about nature too. I'm sure you're going to use the prize money for something like that."

I looked away. I thought my plan to give the money to my parents was a good cause, but even that couldn't seem to compare with Richie's plan.

But if I win, it's my choice what I spend the money on, I remembered. I left Richie by the fire and tried not to let what he said get to me. I had to a big decision to make. It was time to focus.

***

That night, I stood in front of the glowing buttons—orange and yellow—and made the choice of a lifetime.

I returned to the beach and sat down by the fire without looking at either Richie or Diana. Chase paused for dramatic effect before saying, "Going home tonight is . . ." The boat lit up in bright, golden yellow. "Diana!"

She jumped to her feet. "Are you serious? You took Richie over me?"

"I listened to what both of you had to say," I told her. "I think you should go home and become the artist you want to be. Don't try to live up to your dad's expectations."

"That isn't for you to decide!" she yelled. "I wanted to win this competition too. That has nothing to do with my dad. I deserve to stay. I'm the best competitor here."

"If that was true," Richie said quietly, "then you'd be sitting here with me, and Ethan would be the one going home."

Diana's jaw clamped shut. With a final glare at the two of us, she followed Chase onto the boat. The second round was over.

CHAPTER 13

"Thanks for keeping me around," Richie said after the boat had gone. We were alone again at the campsite.

I extinguished the fire. "Don't be too thankful. I almost voted you off."

"I think you made the right decision."

We climbed into the shelter. We lay side by side on the ground, staring up at Amanda's woven ceiling. Outside, a gentle rain began to fall. Water dripped off the corners of the shelter.

"I'm glad for the chance to win," Richie said. "The whole point of me coming on this show was to show my friends back home how easy it is to make it to the end. And I did that."

"Uh-huh," I said.

"Now I just have to win one more time. Should be easy enough."

"Easy?" I turned to him. "I thought you said I outmatched you."

"When it comes to eating bugs, sure. But maybe that's because I don't think eating an enormous spider is worth fifty thousand dollars."

I glared at him. *What is he getting at?*

"Of course, I don't *need* the prize money," Richie continued. "But I definitely want it. My parents' beach house in California is the perfect place to host my eighteenth birthday party. And with fifty thousand dollars to spend, I'm going to make it the greatest party ever!"

"You said you were going to donate the prize money to charity!" I cried, outraged.

Richie shrugged, grinning. "That's what we call a lie, Ethan."

"Why would you lie about something like

that?" I stared at him in disbelief. "That money could really help someone. Instead, you're just going to throw some big party for no reason?"

"My eighteenth birthday is a pretty good reason. Besides, I lied because I knew it would work. All I had to do was pretend to care about nature as much as you do, and you'd take me to the end with you."

"If you don't care, why did you even come on this show?"

Richie laughed mockingly. "You nature-lovers all think you're so special. You think because you care about plants and animals, you have a better chance at winning this competition. But all you need in this game is strength, smarts, and skill. And I have all three."

I gritted my teeth.

Richie turned away from me to go to sleep. "But, if I have to admit it, I'm glad you're my opponent for the final round. You'll be the most fun to beat!"

My jaw dropped open. *I hate this guy!* But even worse, I hated myself for falling for his tricks. I should have known better than to trust him.

The more I thought about it, the more I burned with rage. I prepared myself to do whatever it took to win.

CHAPTER 14

The next morning, Richie and I paced along the shore without a word. Our feet squeaked in the sand. The ocean roared as its waves licked at the beach. Above us, seagulls called out to each other. Despite my growing anticipation, the sounds were beautiful. *I bet Richie doesn't even appreciate them*, I thought bitterly.

When Chase finally arrived, he jumped off the boat and waded to shore holding a huge wooden treasure chest. The lock was solid gold. It sparkled in the sunlight.

Richie's face broke into a horrible grin. "What's that you've got there, Chase?"

"This here," Chase said, "is the grand prize. Inside this chest is fifty thousand dollars for one lucky, talented competitor."

"Can't wait to get my hands on it," Richie replied. He winked at me. I wanted to throw up. On him, preferably.

"You'll notice, of course, that the prize is locked inside of this chest. For the final round, your task is to find a key to unlock it before your opponent does. There are five keys hidden in special golden supply boxes scattered around the island. Each of them will unlock the chest, so you only need to find one. The first one to unlock the chest gets to take home what's inside.

"Most importantly, this round only ends when this chest opens." Chase patted the chest. "That means the round can last anywhere from hours to days. I hope you two are prepared to survive in the wilderness for as long as needed."

This was the ultimate test—one of physical strength, endurance, and strategy.

"Put your hands on the top of the chest

here," Chase commanded. We walked over and did as we were told. "Now, on my count, the final round of this season of *Teen Wilderness Masters* begins. Are you ready?"

I stared out into the trees, trying not to smirk. I already knew where to look—I'd hidden that golden supply box by my shelter in the first round. The problem was going to be remembering where the shelter was. I hadn't revisited it since that round ended.

"On my mark, get set—*go*!" Chase cried.

I tore away from the chest, stumbling in the sand toward the jungle. Richie was close on my heels. Panicking, I thought, *I have to lose him. He can't follow me to the box!*

I ducked through the trees, slowed to a walk, and then quietly circled back to the edge of the jungle. Richie had vanished. Now I could hunt for the stream, which would lead me to my old shelter, and from there I could get the box.

The air was humid, and birdcalls filled my ears. Everything was so still, including me as I drifted along, my footsteps silent. I listened for Richie in the distance but heard no sign of him. *Good.*

I searched for hour after hour to no avail. I found some familiar places, including the two trees where I had outsmarted Peter and the camp where I was caught by Amanda. But, as I kept wandering, I ended up in the middle of nowhere in the jungle, surrounded on all sides by huge flowers and draping vines. The sun was beginning to set, and I was exhausted. I curled up at the base of a tree and went to sleep.

***

I woke up to snorting.

My eyes opened in alarm and there, sniffing at my face, was a wild pig. When it noticed me moving, it squeaked and disappeared into the underbrush.

I sat up, blinking away sleep. The sun was just about to rise, and the sky was a calm gray.

With a rustle, the pig returned, poking its head out of the bushes to stare at me. *Is this the same pig from before?*

I stood up and went over to it, but it darted into the trees. I decided to follow it. Maybe it would lead me to the stream. With every step I took, hope swelled in my chest.

I chased the pig through the jungle until we reached a familiar place—the clearing full of berry bushes and the pile of rocks where the pig lived. The pig ducked into the cave at the base of the pile.

I looked around and grinned. I knew how to find my way from here. The stream was close by. And that meant the box was too. Sure enough, after a few minutes of walking, I heard the telltale sign of water rumbling over rocks. *The stream!*

When I reached it, I knelt down beside it and refiled my canteen. Then, I walked upstream to the rocky overhang.

I sat down in my old camp to rest for a moment. The sticks I had used for a campfire were still here. In the soft dirt around me, there were only my footprints. No sign of Richie.

I stood up and crossed the stream. I found

the box where I had buried it during the first round. Glittering. Unopened. The lock gone. *This is it!*

I yanked the box from its hiding place. It practically sprang open on its own, revealing a beautiful golden skeleton key. I picked it up gingerly, as if it might break if I squeezed too hard. My heart pounded and my fingers tingled with excitement. *I'm going to win. I'm going to take home the prize!*

Suddenly, the sun was blocked by a huge shadow. I turned around and my excitement vanished. My heart thudded to a complete stop. I nearly dropped the key.

Standing on top of the rocky overhang, looking down at me with a triumphant grin was Richie.

CHAPTER 15

"I knew you would lead me to the key," Richie sneered. He spread his arms wide, like he was trying to block my way. "As soon as the challenge started, you seemed to know exactly where to go. I watched you—you were looking too closely to be just hoping to come across a box. All I had to do was follow you. It was too easy."

He jumped down from the cliff and crossed the stream toward me. I clutched the key tightly to my chest.

Richie held out his hand. "We both know I'm the faster and stronger one of the two of us. You can't outrun me. I'll get that key from you way before you even make it back to the beach. You might as well just hand it over now, Ethan."

I pursed my lips.

"Heck, I'll even throw in a little added bonus for you. Give me the key, and I'll give you a thousand dollars for your trouble. Donate it to whatever charity you want." He gave a smug chuckle.

Some bugs buzzed in my ears.

"All right," I said. "I'll give you the key." I held it out in front of me.

Richie grinned and sauntered up to me. "Thanks for making this easy, Ethan."

He leaned in for the key.

In a flash, I yanked it backward, out of his reach. Startled, he leaned over too far and lost his balance.

"Psych!" I cried. I jumped over him and raced across the stream.

He scrambled to his feet and charged after me.

I bolted into the depths of the jungle. My

feet pounded into the dirt, thudding as fast as my heartbeat. The humid air clung to me as I ran. Behind me came Richie's concentrated panting. It was so loud in my ears, louder than the birds and my own breathing. *He's too close!* He would catch me any moment now.

I burst out of the trees into a clearing I knew—a small clearing home to a certain pig. It looked up from the berries it was eating and squealed with surprise. At the last second, I leaped over it.

Then, there was a scream. But not a pig's scream—a boy's scream. I glanced over my shoulder and saw Richie cowering with his arms over his head while the pig bolted into the forest. I couldn't believe it—Richie wasn't a tough guy after all.

I tore out of the clearing, leaving Richie behind. *So much for a love of nature not being an important skill in this game, huh, Richie?* I laughed as I ran. The jungle flew by so fast it was a single smear of green, with flashes of white and yellow and even red as I scared birds into the air.

Then, in the distance, the beach came into view. The ocean was a sparkling blue line running behind the trees. Chase's boat popped up as I got closer. And the chest, its lock twinkling like a star.

"Ethan!" A voice roared from behind me, startling me. Richie had caught up to me.

I broke out from the jungle and into the sunlight and sand. For a moment, I was blinded by the bright white light. Richie jumped out soon after. I felt his fingertips swiping at me. I blinked hard and saw Chase staring at me, open-mouthed. The chest was mere yards ahead of me. I was going to make it. I was going to win!

Richie's fingers grasped at my shirt.

I dove for the chest, ripping out of Richie's grip.

"No!" he shouted. He dove after me.

The two of us flew through the air, me reaching for the lock and Richie reaching for the key. My hand slammed into the chest. The key plunged into the lock. And with a click, the chest popped open, right as Richie and I hit the ground.

"Ethan has opened the chest, and with that, he wins this season of *Teen Wilderness Masters*!" Chase cried. "What an incredible final round!"

I pulled myself to my feet and looked into the chest. On top of a gold plaque reading "Teen Wilderness Master" was a check for $50,000. I couldn't believe it. Behind me, Richie pounded his fist into the sand.

"Congratulations!" Chase took my hand and shook it vigorously.

Dazed, I accepted the chest from him. I had really done it. I was the Teen Wilderness Master!

ABOUT THE AUTHOR

D. A. Graham divides his time between writing and wishing he was writing. He lives in Minneapolis, Minnesota, with his boyfriend and an assortment of foster cats.

REALITY SHOW

ESCAPE!

The ISLAND

THE ONE

The RIGHT NOTE

TREASURE HUNT

WARRIOR ZONE

SUDDENLY ROYAL

Becoming Prince Charming

Family Business

Next in Line

A Noble Cause

Royal Pain

Royal Treatment

THE VALMONTS ARE NOT YOUR TYPICAL ROYAL FAMILY.